DRUMS, KEYBOARDS, AND OTHER INSTRUMENTS

Scott Witmer

VISIT US AT
WWW.ABDOPUBLISHING.COM

Published by ABDO Publishing Company, 8000 West 78th Street, Suite 310, Edina, MN 55439. Copyright ©2010 by Abdo Consulting Group, Inc. International copyrights reserved in all countries. No part of this book may be reproduced in any form without written permission from the publisher. ABDO & Daughters™ is a trademark and logo of ABDO Publishing Company.

Printed in the United States.

 PRINTED ON RECYCLED PAPER

Editor: John Hamilton
Graphic Design: Sue Hamilton
Cover Design: John Hamilton
Cover Photo: Getty Images
Interior Photos and Illustrations: AP-pgs 14, 16, 17, 18, 22, & 23; Getty Images-pgs 5, 7, 9, 11, 12, 13, 15, 19, 24, 25, 26, 28, & 29; iStockphoto-pgs 1, 8, 10, 14, 27, & 31; and Jupiterimages-pgs 3, 4, 6, 14, 21, & 24; RavenFire Media-pg 21, and Yamaha-pg 20.

Library of Congress Cataloging-in-Publication Data

Witmer, Scott.
   Drums, keyboards, and other instruments / Scott Witmer.
      p. cm. -- (Rock band)
   Includes index.
   ISBN 978-1-60453-690-4
   1. Rock groups--Juvenile literature. 2. Musical instruments--Juvenile literature. I. Title.
   ML3534.W613 2009
   786'.19--dc22
                              2009006607

CONTENTS

DRUMS

People have been banging on drums since the beginning of civilization, perhaps as far back as 6,000 BC. Early people used drums, or percussion, for communication, warfare, and religious ceremonies. Drums were used to send messages over long distances because of their loud sound and easily identifiable pitch.

The technical term for a drum is "membranophone." This refers to the membrane of the drum that is stretched over a hollow body. The membrane is struck with a solid object, usually a rounded or curved stick. The membrane vibrates against the body of the drum, producing a loud, distinct sound. This membrane is commonly referred to as the drum "head."

Early drumheads were animal skins that were dried and stretched over the drum body. Animal skins, such as leather, were used on most drums until the 1950s. Modern drumheads are usually made of thins sheets of damage-resistant plastic. Plastic drumheads are much cheaper to produce. They are also much easier to maintain, and need to be replaced less often.

The sound of a drum can be changed by adjusting the size and shape of the body that the drumhead is stretched across. A larger body produces a lower, louder sound. A smaller body results in a brighter, higher sound.

> Early drums were made by stretching animal skins tightly over a hollow-bodied object, such as a clay pot.

Drummer Zach Velmer of Sound Tribe Sector 9 (STS9) performing at a music festival.

There are several types of drums used in music today, but most can be broken down into categories. A typical set of drums, or drum kit, will include the following:

The bass drum, or "kick drum," is the largest. It produces a deep, low-pitched sound. It is most often struck with a floor pedal that is operated by a musician's foot. In marching bands, the bass drum is mounted vertically, and struck on both sides with large padded sticks.

BASS DRUM

The snare drum is constructed with two heads, one on top and another on the bottom of a rounded shell. The name "snare" comes from the bands of metal (or other material) stretched across one of the heads, usually at the bottom. When one head is struck, the metal snares vibrate, producing a bright, dry sound. In modern percussion, the snare is widely considered to be the most important drum. The snare drum is most often played as the "accent" drum, or the drum that keeps a steady beat.

SNARE DRUM

Toms, or tom-tom drums, are medium-sized drums, between the snare and bass drums. The toms are constructed much like snare drums, with two heads. They do not have a "snare" across one of the membranes, however. They are most often used to compliment the percussive sounds of the snare and bass drums, to offer more variety in the drum rhythm. Accomplished indie drummer Brett Gerstenberger, who played in such bands as The Waxed Tadpoles, King King, and Supraluxx, once said, "The kick and snare are for the beat. The toms are for color and texture."

Drummer Dave Agoglia of Rev Theory performing in Columbus, Ohio. Base drums sometimes display the name of the band.

> Drummers can create different sounds from a cymbal depending on the type of cymbal and where it's struck.

Although not technically considered drums, cymbals are a very important part of any percussion section. A cymbal is a thin metal plate that is normally round. The cymbal is struck with a stick, which makes a loud, metallic "crash" sound. Modern cymbals are mounted on a post, or stand. Drummers can create different sounds from a cymbal depending on where they strike it.

The crash cymbal is named for the loud ringing sound it makes when struck. Crash cymbals are normally wide, metal cymbals with a thin, flat edge. The thin edge allows the crash cymbal to continue vibrating for a long time after being struck. Crash cymbals come in different sizes, but modern rock drummers usually use a diameter of about 18 inches (46 cm). Ride cymbals are larger variations of the crash cymbal, and are typically much thicker.

Hi-hats are a combination of two cymbals that are mounted together on top of each other. The hi-hat has a floor pedal that is used to bring the two cymbals together. Hi-hats can be struck "open," with the cymbals apart, or "closed," with the floor pedal pressed and with both cymbals together. Playing the hi-hat open or closed produces two distinctly different sounds.

Normally, the hi-hat is struck in time with the music, which keeps the beat. The crash and ride cymbals are struck for accent within the rhythm.

> Danny Carey of the Grammy Award-winning band Tool. Carey is a skilled musician who varies both the intensity and sound styles of his drumming.

THE DRUM KIT

Early drums were each played separately in concert, with a different person playing each kind of drum. Sometime in the early 1900s, American and European drummers experimented by putting different drum types together to form drum "kits." American inventor William F. Ludwig produced the first practical bass drum pedal system in 1909. With the invention of the drum kit, percussionists could play several types of drums at once, using both arms and legs.

Crash Cymbal

Hi-Hat

Toms

Snare Drum

Throne

Crash Cymbal

Bass Drum

DRUM KIT

Traditional drum kits include a bass drum, a snare, two to three toms, a hi-hat, and one or more crash and ride cymbals. Two tom-tom drums are usually mounted to the bass drum on brackets. The hi-hat, crash cymbal, larger "floor" tom, and snare drum are on separate stands situated around the bass drum. The drummer typically sits on a round stool, or "throne." A drum throne normally swivels for easy movement, and has an adjustable height.

The drum kit for the band Judas Priest on stage.

> Meg White of The White Stripes uses a minimalist drum kit.

As rock and roll music became more popular in the 1960s and 1970s, drum kits became more and more extravagant. Drummers began adding more and more cymbals, toms, and other percussive instruments to their kits. Some drummers added additional kick drums, so that two bass beats could be played faster.

In the 1980s, percussionists began experimenting with electronic drums, which produced a variety of digital sounds that could be manipulated, much like keyboard synthesizers. However, with the resurgence of "garage rock" and "indie rock" in the 1990s and early part of the 21st century, many rock bands and drummers returned to basic stripped-down, five-piece drum kits.

Regardless of the size of the drum kit used, the drummer's role in a rock band is a very important one. The drummer's job is to "keep time," maintaining a constant tempo for each song. Tempo is measured in beats per minute, or BPM. The higher the BPM, the faster the tempo, or speed, of the song. Most rock bands follow the tempo and rhythm provided by the drummer. This makes the percussionist the key to keeping songs sounding steady. So, even though the drummer and the drum kit are normally placed in the back of the stage, they are key to any rock band's success.

Neil Peart of the rock band Rush is considered one of the best drummers in the world. He has an extravagant drum kit.

OTHER PERCUSSION INSTRUMENTS

In addition to standard drum kits, rock bands often use other percussion instruments to add variety or an exotic sound to the music. A gong is a huge cymbal suspended on a frame. Wind chimes are very small metal cylinders that are rung together to produce a light, airy sound. Shakers, maracas, and vibroslaps are small handheld instruments used to create distinctive sound effects to accent the rhythm section.

A tambourine is a hand-held instrument, similar to a small drum, which is played by slapping one hand against the drumhead. In the 1980s, the band Violent Femmes famously used a xylophone on the classic song "Gone Daddy Gone."

The use of non-traditional percussion sound effects is very effective to emphasize certain passages of a song. These instruments can add color, variety, and even humor into an otherwise bland section.

David Sitek of the rock band TV on the Radio performing with wind chimes hanging from his guitar.

Maracas

Tambourines

Xylophone

Wayne Coyne of the Flaming Lips performing onstage using a gong. The Zildjian Company produces a number of percussion instruments used by both amateur and professional musicians. The company states that their gongs produce a complex blend of highs and lows, with beautiful warm overtones and plenty of attack when necessary.

VOCALS AND PA

Singers use an instrument that everyone has, but very few know how to use. That instrument is their voice. The vocalist in a band has a very important job. Almost every rock and roll song has lyrics. The words to a song are normally what we relate to, what we remember most. Imagine your favorite rock song. Now imagine that same song without any lyrics. That's hard to do, isn't it?

It has been said, "singers are born, not trained." However, in rock music that is not necessarily true. There are many rock superstars who have been criticized for not having great voices, but who sell millions of records. Patrick Stump of Fall Out Boy, Scott Stapp of Creed, Madonna, Gwen Stefani of No Doubt, and even Bono of U2 have all been criticized for their less-than-perfect vocal delivery. However, in rock music, it is more important to have a good delivery and something to say rather than a pitch-perfect voice. Singing on key is important, but being perfect has never been what rock and roll is all about.

Lead singer Patrick Stump (center) of Fall Out Boy has been criticized for his singing.

> Gwen Stefani of No Doubt was once told she had a "loopy, unpredictable" voice.

17

Vocalists have many roles in a rock band. First, of course, they perform the vocals. But singers are also oftentimes considered the "lead" person in the band. The singer projects the band's personality, and is often called the "front man" or "front woman." This is a difficult position for many singers to be in, especially when band members contribute equally to

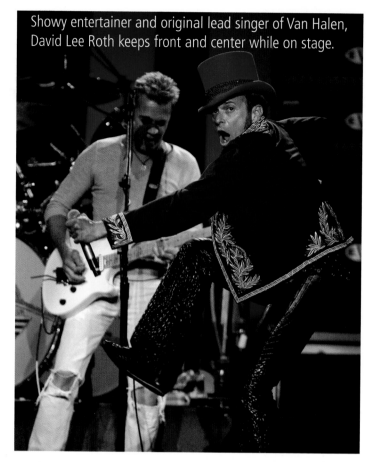

Showy entertainer and original lead singer of Van Halen, David Lee Roth keeps front and center while on stage.

the songwriting. For every spotlight-stealing lead singer, like David Lee Roth of Van Halen, there are just as many gracious singers who attempt to deflect attention back to the band, like Coldplay's Chris Martin. Singers must have self-confidence, but out-of-control egos can be destructive to bands.

In a live performance, a singer's voice is amplified by a PA, or public address system. PA systems usually include one or more amplifiers, at least one speaker, and at least one microphone. Along with the amplifier, PA systems usually have an equalizer attached. An equalizer is an electronic device that allows sound to be adjusted, or modified. Electronic effects can also be added. These may include a reverb effect, which adds an echo sound, or a delay effect, which adds a more dramatic repeating echo sound. PA systems usually include monitors, which are speakers pointed backward so the musicians on stage can hear the vocals.

Coldplay's Chris Martin and Jonny Buckland share the stage.

19

A basic Yamaha all-in-one portable PA with a mixer and speakers.

PA systems vary greatly in size, performance, and price. An entry-level PA system is usually an "all-in-one" box that includes an amplifier, equalizer, and basic effects. This inexpensive system usually includes a few speakers for the audience, and maybe one monitor. It is ideal for band practice spaces, or for performances at smaller venues.

As venues become larger, PA systems become more expensive and elaborate. Higher-end PA systems have components that are mounted horizontally in a case, or "rack." These systems are usually owned by the venue where the concert takes place. Most touring bands do not need to haul a PA system from place to place—it is normally provided by the concert hall. Sometimes, however, superstar acts have huge, custom PA systems. They are operated by several sound technicians, and are moved from place to place as the band tours.

> Many concert halls have their own public address (PA) system, so performers do not have to travel from place to place with all their own heavy and expensive equipment.

HOW A MICROPHONE WORKS

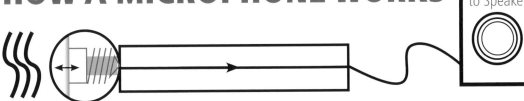

Amplifier to Speaker

Sound waves strike a diaphragm (blue), making it move back and forth. A coil (red) attached to the diaphram vibrates as well. A magnet (orange) produces a magnetic field that surrounds the coil. As the coil vibrates through the magnetic field, an electric current flows. The electric current flows to an amplifier, where the sound is increased, or amped up. It then goes to a speaker.

A very important part of a PA system is the microphone. It is the originating point for the sound that the vocalist makes. A microphone works in the exact opposite way that a speaker does. When sound vibrates an electric coil in the head of the microphone, it is converted to an electronic signal, which is sent to an amplifier. This weak signal is then strengthened, or amplified, and sent to speakers. There are hundreds of different microphone models and styles in production today. The type of microphone that any vocalist uses usually comes down to personal preference. The nicer, more accurate microphones can be very expensive. The type of PA system a band chooses usually comes down to budget, power needs, and convenience.

> There are many different types of microphones. Some are hand-held, some rest in a stand, and others are hands-free, wrapping around a person's head. There are also many different quality and expense levels.

CLASSICAL INSTRUMENTS

Normally, when someone thinks about rock and roll instruments, they think about guitars and drums. While these instruments are most certainly commonplace in rock bands today, other instruments have recently made a resurgence. Classical instruments that are normally used in orchestras are often heard in rock music. Classical instruments add a fresh, new sound to rock and roll. The use of classical instruments in rock is limited only by an artist's creative imagination.

In the 1950s, Jerry Lee Lewis was famous for his hard-rocking piano playing, especially his hit song "Great Balls of Fire."

The piano has always had a place in rock and roll. Little Richard and Jerry Lee Lewis famously banged their keys in the 1950s. In the 1960s through the 1980s, the piano was often used for ballads and slower songs. Famous examples include "Let It Be" by The Beatles, "Can't Fight This Feeling" by REO Speedwagon, and "Come Sail Away" by Styx. In the late 1990s and earlier part of the 2000s, rock bands began using piano as a main instrument in uptempo rock songs. Coldplay is a famous example. With the commercial success of Coldplay, other bands have followed suit, including One Republic, Ben Folds Five, The Fray, and Jack's Mannequin.

Coldplay's Chris Martin playing piano.

> Many rock and roll bands use the piano in their music.

Front man Andrew McMahon is the piano player for the group Jack's Mannequin.

> Boyd Tinsley of the Dave Mathews Band performing on stage with his violin.

Stringed instruments have been used in rock for decades. Normally, strings have made special appearances, not played by regular members of the band. However, as alternative and indie rock bands have experimented with different sounds, instruments such as violins and cellos have made their way into rock. The Dave Mathews Band features a violinist, as do indie rock darlings The Decemberists.

Violins have been used in rock music for many decades, although usually in special songs.

The cello is the "big brother" of the violin. It is a large, stringed instrument with a very distinct, lower tone. Indie rock band Cursive toured with a cellist placed in the center of the stage, and the cello sound was incorporated heavily into several of their albums. Apocalyptica is a three-piece band of cellists from Finland. They play heavy metal music with three cellists and one drummer, and have opened for such metal superstars as Metallica and Rammstein.

> Perttu Kivilaakso is one of three cellists and a drummer from Finland called Apocalyptica. The group is famous for playing Metallica songs on their cellos.

BIG BAND INSTRUMENTS

Brass, or big band, instruments have had a long presence in rock and popular music. Brass instruments include trumpets, trombones, and related instruments. Saxophones, clarinets, and flutes belong to the woodwind family, but are included in the big band instrument group as well.

Saxophones were used heavily by bar bands in the late 1970s and 1980s, and saxophone solos were commonplace in rock music during the 1980s. Clarence Clemons, who plays with Bruce Springsteen and the E Street Band, is perhaps the most famous saxophonist in rock and roll. His roaring sax solos and enormous stage presence became the E Street Band's trademark.

E Street Band's Clarence Clemons on saxophone performs with lead singer Bruce Springsteen on guitar.

Saxophones are often heard in jazz music, but are also played in rock and roll.

ROCK SAXOPHONIST

> Lead singer and flutist Ian Anderson creates many memorable flute parts for the rock band Jethro Tull.

One of the most famous uses of the flute to ever be recorded on a rock and roll album was heard on Jethro Tull's masterpiece "Aqualung." The lead singer and flutist, Ian Anderson, is widely regarded as playing the most memorable flute parts in rock.

Bands such as the Squirrel Nut Zippers and Big Bad Voodoo Daddy brought an entire brass and woodwind ensemble to their band lineup. They infused a danceable swing sound into their rock music. These swing rock bands became very popular in the 1990s.

> Big Bad Voodoo Daddy uses many different brass, woodwind, and stringed instruments to create their music. Alto and baritone saxophones, alto and tenor clarinets, trumpets, trombone, piano, drums, bass, guitar, and vocals combine to create the driving swing music that has made the group so popular.

GLOSSARY

BPM - BEATS PER MINUTE

How fast or slow a piece of music is based on the number of beats that happen in a period of 60 seconds (one minute).

DELAY EFFECT

An electronic effect that creates a dramatic, repeating, echo sound.

FRONT MAN / FRONT WOMAN

The person who acts as a group's leader. This is often the lead singer.

MEMBRANOPHONE

Historically, the technical word used for a drum.

PERCUSSION

Instruments used to create a beat, such as drums, cymbals, xylophones, gongs, bells, rattles, wind chimes, and more. Percussion sounds are usually created by striking the instrument with the hand or a stick, or by shaking the instrument.

PITCH

The highness or lowness of a sound. A singer or musician whose voice or instrument is off-key is sometimes said to be "pitchy." A person who always sings or plays in tune is said to have "perfect pitch."

REVERB

Short for reverberation, this is an electronic effect that adds an echo sound.

Rhythm

The regular, repeated pattern, or beats, in a piece of music.

Tempo

The speed at which a piece of music is played. Tempo is often referred to in Italian terms, such as *allegro* (fast), *moderato* (moderate), and *adagio* (slow).

Throne

The seat on which a drummer sits. It usually swivels to allow the drummer easy access to all the instruments being played.

Woodwind

A type of musical instrument that creates sound when a person blows air at the edge of, or into an opening in, the instrument. Flutes, oboes, clarinets, saxophones, and bassoons are all woodwind instruments.

The drummer's job is to "keep time," maintaining a constant rhythm for each song. A skilled drummer will be both an anchor and a propeller—keeping time as well as moving a song forward.

INDEX